You Can Recycle!

Julie Haydon

Contents

Garbage 2
You Can Recycle! 6
Recycling Organic Material 8
Recycling Paper 10
Recycling Other Things 12
Helping the Environment 14
Glossary and Index 16

Rigby

Garbage

What happens
to the garbage
you put
in the bin?

Trucks collect the garbage.
The garbage goes to a **landfill site**.

Then it is dumped
into a big hole
in the ground
and buried.

3

Over time, some of the buried garbage breaks down and rots.
This can **pollute** the air, water, and land.

Sometimes garbage is burned.
This can pollute the air, too.

You Can Recycle!

Recycle your garbage.

This will help keep the **environment** clean.

Recycling garbage means using it again or making something new from it.

aluminum cans

plastic bottles and bags

glass jars and bottles

You can recycle all of this garbage!

cardboard

newspapers and magazines

food scraps

dust

Recycling Organic Material

Organic material was once part of a plant or animal.

You can recycle organic material by putting it in a **compost** bin.

The organic material will rot
and turn into compost.
Compost is good for your garden.

Recycling Paper

Paper is made
from wood.
Wood comes from trees.
Recycling paper
can save trees
from being cut down.

You can put old paper
into recycling bins.
The old paper will be recycled
to make new paper.

Recycling Other Things

You can recycle glass jars and bottles, aluminum cans, plastic bottles, and bags.

Clean them and put them in recycling bins.

Some things will be cleaned and reused.

Other things will go to factories.
They will be made into new **products**.

new
products

Helping the Environment

You can help
the environment
by recycling.
Recycle as much as you can!

Glossary

aluminum	a light metal
compost	what organic material turns into when it breaks down
environment	the land, water, and air around us
landfill site	where garbage is dumped and buried
organic material	anything that was once part of an animal or plant. Food scraps, dead flowers, and dust are organic material.
pollute	to make dirty
products	things that have been made
recycle	to reuse something or to make something new from it

Index

aluminum 7, 12
compost 8, 9
dust 7
environment 6, 14–15
food scraps 7

glass 7, 12
landfill site 3
organic 8–9
paper 7, 10–11
plastic 7, 12

pollute 4–5
products 13
garbage 2–3, 4–5, 6–7
trees 10